HUMPHREY, the Dancing Pig

THE DIAL PRESS

New York

HUMPHREY,
THE DANCING PIG

STORY AND PICTURES BY

ARTHUR GETZ

Published by The Dial Press
1 Dag Hammarskjold Plaza
New York, New York 10017

Copyright © 1980 by Arthur Getz
Designed by Jane Byers Bierhorst | First printing

The art for each picture consists of a black ink
line-drawing and four halftone separations.

Library of Congress Cataloging
in Publication Data

Getz, Arthur.
Humphrey, the dancing pig.

Summary | In his desire to be slim
like the cat, Humphrey the pig
dances his weight away.

[1. Pigs—Fiction.
2. Weight control—Fiction.
3. Dancing—Fiction] I. Title.
PZ7.G3298Hu   [E]   79-20616
ISBN 0-8037-4496-X
ISBN 0-8037-4497-8 lib. bdg.

To Madeline and Anthony

Humphrey was a pretty pink curly-tailed pig.

He lived in a barnyard with a cat, an old horse, a milking cow, a sheep, a family of chickens, and a family of ducks.

One day Humphrey wandered down to the duck pond and took a good look at his reflection in the water. Humphrey thought, "Why can't I be slim? I don't like the way I look. I will dance until I am slim as the cat."

Humphrey walked back to the barnyard and began to skip around in a big circle.

All day long he skipped and skipped. The red hen told her chicks to stay out of Humphrey's way.

Early the next morning he took another look at himself in the duck pond. Then he spent the day practicing kicks. The horse and a cowbird watched Humphrey as he kicked, up and down, up and down.

Every morning Humphrey looked at himself in the duck pond, and every night he went to bed near the cow stall. He dreamed he was getting slimmer.

As soon as he woke up, Humphrey began to dance. He did a different dance every day.

One day he did a cossack dance. It was hard work.

Humphrey did Indian dancing,

rock 'n' roll,

and then ballet.

He did acrobatic dancing

and also hula dancing.

Humphrey even did a whirling dervish dance. Around and around he went like a top. Then one morning . . .

the farmer asked the cow, "Who is that stranger in my barn?"

"That is no stranger—that is Humphrey, the Dancing Pig.
Humphrey likes to be thin—like the cat."

"Put that pig to work," the farmer said. "If he wants to be like the cat, make him catch mice and rats."

From that day on Humphrey had to run back and forth, chasing after mice and rats. The cat began to get fat. Humphrey got thinner and thinner.

"Goodness," Humphrey said. "Look how fat that lazy cat is getting. And I am doing all of his work. All he does is eat and sleep. I quit!"

He went back to the corncrib and found a big ear of corn. "How good it tastes," thought Humphrey as he sat down. "I'll have another."

Every day he ate until he could eat no more, and every night he slept on top of his pile of corn.

The cat had to go back to chasing mice,

and Humphrey became his old self again. "What a very beautiful pig he is," the farmer said. The cow, the horse, the sheep, the ducks, and the chickens agreed.

But the cat wasn't so sure.